Bodhi's BELIZEAN Adventures

Anju Ganglani

Bodhi's BELIZEAN Adventure?

@2024 by Anju Ganglani

ISBN: 9798879260007

Email: WordsbyAnjuGang@gmail.com

Dedication

This book is dedicated to my fellow Belizeans. I lived in Belize for 18 years of my life. It will forever be my 'first love'. My childhood was filled with the amazing memories of beautiful sites and wonderful people. This book is dedicated to all my Belizean family and friends!
Ya da fu we Belize!

Let me introduce you to ME.

I'm **Bodhi**, beautiful **Belizean bird** you'll see..

I'm an exotic toucan, native to Belize,

In fact I'm the national bird, would you believe?

I'll take you on an adventure together, come.

As we explore Belize, you're welcome!

WELCOME

Firstly, you ask, Belize – where is this?

It's a country you really need to visit.

In a land of wonders, where the sun always gleams,
There lies a gem of a beauty, a land of bright dreams.

In Central America this jewel can be seen,
Nestled in the heart of the Caribbean.

To the north we have friendly Mexico!
To the west lies Guatemala, our neighbor so.

GUATEMALA

In what languages are Belizean stories told?

We speak English, Spanish and our Creole.

The Great Barrier Reef, it is the 2nd largest reef in the world!

Home to hundreds of species of coral, fish and marine mammals so bold.

People come from near and far, just to snorkel and dive,

Experience the wonders under the sea, gleaming and alive,

Belize's islands are known as the Cayes,
Tourists flock here to sunbathe by the sea.

Walk barefoot and enjoy the stunning islands,

Keep your feet wet or enjoy the lush dry land.

Gentle waves caress the shore inviting you to play

In the land where the sun shines bright both night and day.

Taste the yummy Belizean cuisine,

Panades & tamales, & our staple rice and beans.

Drink fresh coconut water, enjoy and chill.

Soak it all in, at home you'll feel.

Some of the most beautiful animals can be admired here.

From dolphins to butterflies, toucans and tapirs.

The wildlife of Belize, so diverse and grand.

From the jaguar's stealthy stride to the toucan's vibrant band.

Butterflies dance in the air, with colors bright and bold.

And howler monkeys sing their songs, their voices never old.

Have you seen a picture of the world famous Blue Hole?

This diving wonder is the largest sized hole in the world.

1000 feet in circumference and more than 400 feet deep!

This UNESCO Heritage Site is one we safely keep.

Mayan ruins stand proud, a testament of the past,

With pyramids that reach the sky, memories that last.

Step back in time, imagine days of old,

As you walk amongst the ruins, stories will unfold

Discover nature's wonders, explore with wide-eyed glee

For Belize is a magical land, where beauty truly thrives, you see.

Embrace the golden beaches, the jungles' verdant green

With every step you take, a new adventure will be seen.

Belize holds treasures far and wide,

So come and seek its beauty, let Bodhi be your guide!

Meet the Author

Anju Ganglani is the headmistress of Prime Primary School in Kano, Nigeria. She has worked in Education for the past 18 years. She grew up in Belize, studied in Canada, worked in India and now lives in Nigeria. She has a Master's Degree in Educational Psychology. Writing poems and short stories is her passion. She believes that words have the ability to move the 'mountains' in our hearts.

Made in the USA
Columbia, SC
23 December 2024

48262773R00020